PUPPY PATROL ™

BOOMERANG BOB

BOOKS IN THE PUPPY PATROL™ SERIES

COMING SOON

BOOMERANG BOB

JENNY DALE

Illustrations by Mick Reid
Cover illustration by Michael Rowe

AN
APPLE
PAPERBACK

SCHOLASTIC INC.
New York Toronto London Auckland Sydney
Mexico City New Delhi Hong Kong Buenos Aires

No part of this publication may be reproduced, in whole or in part, or stored in a retrieval system, or transmitted in any form or by any means, electronic, mechanical, photocopying, recording, or otherwise, without written permission of the publisher. For information regarding permission, write to Macmillan Publishers Ltd., 20 New Wharf Rd., London N1 9RR Basingstoke and Oxford.

ISBN 0-439-45348-8

All rights reserved. Published by Scholastic Inc., 557 Broadway, New York, NY 10012 by arrangement with Macmillan Children's Books, a division of Macmillan Publishers Ltd.

SCHOLASTIC and associated logos are trademarks and/or registered trademarks of Scholastic Inc.

12 11 10 9 8 7 6 5 4 3   6 7 8/0

Printed in the U.S.A.   40
First Scholastic printing, May 2003

SPECIAL THANKS TO LORNA READ

CHAPTER ONE

"This is your captain speaking."

The Parker family stopped talking and paid attention to the smooth voice coming over the airplane's intercom. The five of them were sitting in the center row of a jumbo jet that had flown nonstop from England to Australia. It felt as if they'd been in the air forever.

"We'll soon be starting our descent to Sydney's Kingsford Smith Airport," continued the pilot. "The temperature on the ground is a very pleasant 29 degrees Celsius — that's 84 degrees Fahrenheit. Local time is a little after four in the afternoon on Monday, December 27th."

"I want to go to the beach!" exclaimed five-year-old

Sarah Parker, bouncing up and down on her seat by the aisle.

"Calm down, Squirt!" Her older brother, Neil, exchanged amused glances with his other sister, ten-year-old Emily. "You're making me feel hot already."

"Yeah, good thing I brought my flip-flops." Emily laughed. "Australia is going to be boiling!"

Carole Parker, their mother, smiled, too. "I bet it's freezing at home. Compton is probably under three feet of snow!"

Neil turned to his father. "I hope everything's OK back at King Street Kennels," he said anxiously.

"Of course it will be," Bob Parker replied heartily. He fastened his seat belt, ready for the descent. "Bev and Kate will both be in every day, and Uncle Jack never lets us down."

The Parkers ran a busy dog rescue center in the countryside just outside the small town of Compton. Kate McGuire and Bev Mitchell were their two dedicated kennel assistants, who cared as much about dog welfare as Neil and Emily did. Jack Tansley was Carole's brother. He was staying at their house to look after the day-to-day running of King Street Kennels while the Parker family was on the other side of the world.

"I've told Kate to make sure that Jake gets plenty of walks," Neil said. "You know what a bundle of energy he is." Jake was his young Border collie. "I'm missing him already," he added.

"So am I." Emily sighed.

"Jake will be fine," their mother said. "And you un-grateful kids are about to have the best vacation of your lives!"

Bob Parker's great-aunt Victoria, who'd lived in Australia for many years, had died that year. Like all the Parkers, Victoria had been a great dog lover, and she'd left Bob enough money to build the new rescue center at King Street. Neil and his family were all very thankful for the inheritance, and now they were on their way to visit her grave. They were also going to meet Viola, the old lady who'd been Victoria's friend for many years and who was living in Victoria's old house outside of Sydney.

"We've got a lot to fit in during the next eight days," said Carole cheerfully. "But I'm sure we'll manage it all once we've settled in."

The family had rented a bungalow in Dingo Bay, a beach in Sydney's northern suburbs.

"All I want is to see a Kelpie and a Blue Heeler," Neil said eagerly. "The Australian breeds sound so cool."

"What sort of dog did you say Sporty was?" Emily asked her father. Sporty had been Great-Aunt Victoria's dog, and Viola was now taking care of him. Emily and Neil were looking forward to meeting them both the following day — after the family had recovered from their marathon journey.

Before Bob Parker could reply, there was a series

of bumps and a deafening roar as the jet's brakes came on.

They had touched down.

Neil and Emily couldn't help cheering — they were in Australia for the very first time!

Bob Parker stood in the arrivals hall scanning a stack of papers he'd taken out of an envelope. It was a bright, bustling space filled with shops, banks, and information centers. "I need to find out where to pick up our rental car," he said. "If you guys wouldn't mind staying here till I get back . . ."

As he strolled off, Sarah tugged her mother's sleeve. "Mom, Mom, there's a koala!" she squealed, pointing at a nearby gift shop. "Isn't it cute? Can I have one?" she begged.

"I'll come with you," said Emily, gazing in the same direction. "It looks like they've got some great backpacks in there."

"Neil, would you mind keeping an eye on the bags?" asked Carole. "We'll only be gone a couple of minutes."

"No prob." Neil leaned back against the suitcases and looked around. He felt ridiculously overdressed in the jeans and jacket he'd worn on the plane. Everyone else seemed to be in shorts and T-shirts. And they were all so tan!

His dad's guidebook said that the state of New

South Wales had some of the best surfing beaches in the world. Neil sighed in anticipation. Some surf carnivals — in which the local lifesaving clubs displayed their skills by competing against one another in a variety of beach events — were going on right now. Not only was Neil looking forward to watching them, he was hoping to rent a board and try surfing himself!

"Oops!" a female voice exclaimed.

Neil turned around to see a dark-haired girl of about twelve who was staggering under the weight of an enormous red backpack. She had tripped on one of the Parker's suitcases and was about to drop the canvas tote bag she was carrying. It landed next to Neil.

"My fault," Neil apologized, jolted out of his daydream. "I shouldn't have left that suitcase sticking out like that." He bent down to pick up the girl's bag for her.

"No — leave it!" she snapped in an American accent. The girl snatched up the bag, hugged it to her, and moved quickly away from him.

Neil was dumbstruck. Why was she being so rude when he was only trying to help?

Neil noticed that one of the girl's backpack straps had slipped and needed adjusting. He watched as she glanced around her, then put the tote bag down again while she took off her backpack and adjusted

the strap. Then she crouched down beside the tote bag, pulled the zipper open, and peeked furtively inside.

Neil frowned. *She's behaving very strangely,* he thought. *Almost guiltily, in fact — as if she's got something she shouldn't have in that bag.*

Then Neil heard a faint noise. It sounded a bit like a baby whimpering, but he wasn't sure where it was coming from.

The noise came again. With a shock, Neil realized it was coming from the girl's tote bag. Not only that, but it was a sound he was extremely familiar with!

The girl zipped up the bag and heaved on her backpack. As she bent to pick up the tote, Neil heard a loud, clear yap.

"Hey!" he exclaimed. "Have you got a dog in there?" He stepped forward to block her path.

"Wh . . . what are you talking about?" she stuttered.

"You can't take an animal on a plane. You know that's not allowed. It needs to be in a proper carrier."

The girl looked as though Neil was making her nervous. She shot anxious glances at passers-by. "It's just a toy. One of those walking, talking toy dogs. You can get them in Paddy's Market." She was speaking quickly. "When I dropped the bag, it must have set off the mechanism."

She looked shifty and Neil knew she was lying. "Yeah, right! Open the bag and let me have a look!"

The whimpering began again. "Shhh, Bob," the girl said. Then she looked at Neil, her face flushing scarlet as she realized she'd just given herself away.

"You *do* have a dog in your bag!" Neil said triumphantly.

Tears sprang to the girl's eyes. "Don't tell my parents," she cried desperately. "I've got to take him home to California with me, I've just got to. He doesn't belong to anybody, he's just a little stray, and I love him so much . . ."

"OK, OK." Neil crouched down beside the tote bag. "Let's get him out of there to start with." He unzipped the bag and felt a warm, wet tongue licking his hand.

A shiny black nose poked its way out of the gap, followed by an impish white face with a tan patch

over one eye and matching tan-colored ears. "It's a Jack Russell!" he exclaimed.

The girl burst into tears.

"It's a long flight to America," said Neil as he stroked the terrier's ears. The dog responded and tried to lick Neil even more. "How is he going to get food and water? It's cruel, you know. You can't do it. If you get caught smuggling a dog, you'll get into big trouble and the dog will be confiscated. He'll be put in quarantine, then into a rescue center — you'd never see him again."

"I'm sorry," she wailed. "I thought that, as long as

nobody found him on the plane, it'd be all right. I was going to feed him my in-flight meal, and I've got some potato chips and a bottle of water."

She really is clueless about dogs, Neil thought angrily. *She has no idea at all.*

An announcement came over the loudspeaker: "Would passenger Stacey Thomas on Flight 378 to Los Angeles please come to Check-in Desk 13, where your parents are waiting."

"That's me! I've got to go! I haven't even checked in yet!" the girl cried desperately.

Suddenly, she scooped the small, wriggling dog out of the tote bag and thrust him into Neil's arms. "Here, you take him. Look after him, won't you?"

"What? I can't take him!" protested Neil, turning his head away as the dog tried to lick his nose.

"I found him on the beach in Dingo Bay," the girl said breathlessly. "You see, they've got these new rules about dogs . . ." she called over her shoulder as she hurried away.

"But — but I don't even live here. I'm on vacation, too," said Neil, panicking. "What do you think I'm going to do with a — hey, come back!"

But the girl was gone.

Neil scanned the crowds and eventually picked her out, hurrying toward one of the departure gates. Rooted to the spot with shock, Neil watched as she waved her boarding card at an official and vanished into the departure lounge.

He came to with a jolt as the hairy bundle in his arms tried to squirm free. He gave the small dog a stroke and held him more firmly. "Bob, eh? Well, hello, Bob. What in the world am I going to do with you?" he asked the terrier. Neil had met dogs in strange circumstances before, but this had to be one of the strangest.

Suddenly, he heard his sister Sarah's voice yelling, "Hey, Neil! I've got a koala!"

He looked up. His mother and sisters were coming toward him, followed closely by his father.

As one, they all stopped dead in their tracks and stared at the Jack Russell cradled in his arms.

Sarah's mouth dropped open.

"Neil," said his dad. "I don't believe it! You've done it again!"

Neil flopped back onto the pile of luggage and smiled nervously as the dog did its best to give his nose another lick.

CHAPTER TWO

"**N**eil Parker — can we not leave you alone for five minutes without you finding a dog?" Bob Parker sounded stern, but he was looking quite amused.

Neil shuffled his feet. "I can explain. It's not my fault . . ."

"For once!" mumbled Emily, smirking.

Bob Parker scratched the terrier's head and was rewarded with a lick. "He's a cute little guy, that's for sure, but we haven't got time for this. Put him down now, Neil. I've picked up the car — it's parked outside."

Everybody picked up a suitcase and headed toward the revolving exit doors.

Everybody except Neil.

"It's not as easy as that, Dad . . ." Neil hesitated, wondering how to explain. "I'm stuck with him. *We're* stuck with him."

"What do you mean?" asked Carole.

The girls' new presents were forgotten as everybody crowded around asking questions.

When he'd heard his son's story, Bob Parker scratched his beard. "Well, we can't take him with us," he said firmly. "There's a No Pets rule in our bungalow. The best we can do is hand him over to the airport authorities."

"But, Dad, he's so *sweet*!" Emily cooed, fondling the Jack Russell's folded-over ears. "And I bet he's thirsty after being cooped up in that girl's bag."

"Here, give him some of this," Carole said, producing a bottle of mineral water from her flight bag.

Neil poured some water into the palm of his hand, and the terrier lapped it up eagerly.

"I wonder what your name is, little one?" Emily murmured.

"The American girl called him Bob," said Neil.

They all burst out laughing — especially Bob Parker. "That does it! Two Bobs in this family is one too many! One of us has got to go, and you need this one to drive the car," he reminded them. "Where did the girl say she found him?"

"Dingo Bay," Neil replied.

"That's where we're going," said Carole.

"Hmmm. I suppose we'd better take him back with us, then," said Bob.

"Yippee!" cried Sarah delightedly.

"We'll find a local rescue center where we can hand him in," said Bob. "Neil — that'll be your job. And we'd better make sure to walk him before we drive any distance with him."

"He hasn't got a leash," Emily pointed out.

"We could use one of our luggage straps," Neil suggested. "And we can buy a proper leash tomorrow."

Together Neil and Emily made a temporary collar and leash, then the family left the terminal building to pack their luggage into the big rented Landcruiser.

It was ten miles to Sydney. As they set off, Neil found it hard to concentrate on the buildings flashing by outside his window. He knew he should have been excited about being in Australia, but he was much more concerned about his new companion — Bob the Jack Russell terrier.

Dogs were everything to Neil. It was a stroke of luck that his parents owned a kennel. It meant he could learn about every aspect of looking after dogs *and* have a multitude of canine adventures in the process.

Once they were clear of the airport, Bob Parker took a turn off the freeway and looked for a good place to stop. It wasn't long before he found a recre-

ation area where other people were exercising their
dogs.

As soon as the little dog was let out of the car, he
became a bundle of energy. He bounced, he ran and
yapped, he leaped after flies and tried to catch
them — and he soon had the whole family in
stitches. The funniest thing was the way he would
run away from them in one direction — then whip
around and dash back to them.

"He's just like a boomerang," joked Neil.

"Hey, what a great name for him — Boomerang
Bob!" said Emily. Everyone agreed.

"He's very bright," Neil observed, "and he seems to
trust us. I think he must be used to people."

"That's why Jack Russells make such good work-ing dogs," his father pointed out. "They're highly in-telligent, very energetic, and they get along with everybody."

"Here, Bob," called Sarah, clapping her hands.

Boomerang Bob trotted dutifully toward her, then stopped. He'd spotted another dog racing after a ball thrown by its owner, and he dashed off to join in the chase. This time, it took several shouts and a loud whistle from Bob Parker to bring the speedy little dog back.

"You need some training, Bob," Neil said sternly.

"Now you've seen the not-so-good side of Jack Rus-sells," said his father, laughing. "They're very inquis-itive and easily distracted."

"And rather fond of running away," added Carole. "Perhaps that's how he ended up as a stray."

"Oh, poor little Bob," said Sarah, crouching down and giving him a cuddle.

Bob Parker consulted his watch. "Come on, kids. Let's get on our way. I promised that we'd pick up the bungalow keys around seven o'clock and it's already past six."

They were soon heading for the center of Sydney. Everyone gazed out of the windows as the city flashed by. Boomerang Bob had fallen asleep on Neil's lap, and Neil was beginning to feel a bit sleepy himself when Sarah cried out, "There's the ocean!"

"That's Sydney Harbor," Carole said, "and any minute now we'll be going over Sydney Harbor Bridge. I think we might even be able to see the Opera House."

"I can tell you've done your geography homework, Mom!" Neil joked.

"There it is!" said Carole. They all craned their necks to look at the Opera House, perched at the end of a promontory to the right of the bridge, its famous shells stark white against the early evening sky.

A thrill ran through Neil. For the first time, he really felt as if he were on vacation. The sun was bright, the blue water was dotted with boats, and he had a new doggy friend. Nothing could be better.

When Bob Parker picked up the keys from the real estate agent, he said that there was no need for her to come with them to show them around. Luckily, she didn't insist — they didn't want her discovering Neil's canine companion!

The directions were straightforward, and the family soon reached their vacation destination.

The house was a detached bungalow set in its own lush green gardens. A quiet road separated it from the beach. Directly behind the bungalow was a cliff face festooned with trailing vines.

A pink-and-gray bird flew out of a gum tree, screeching deafeningly.

"It's a parrot!" cried Sarah.

"That's right — it's a kind of parrot called a

galah," said her father. "I remember great-aunt Victoria telling me in one of her letters that galahs and kookaburras are the noisiest birds in Australia!"

Just then, the dog barked loudly.

"He must be thirsty again," Neil said, "and I bet he's hungry, too. Can we go to the store and get him some food?"

"Let's get inside and unpack first," said Carole, opening the front door. "We don't want anyone spotting him."

"I'll get him some water," said Neil, finding his way to the kitchen.

The pots and pans were neatly lined up on a shelf in the spacious cooking area. Neil left the terrier lapping a cool drink and went to look around the rest of the house.

He picked a bedroom on the cliff side of the bungalow. It was cool and shady, which would make it the best place for him and Boomerang Bob to sleep. Even if the feisty little dog was only going to be with them for a day or so, there was no way Neil wanted to be parted from him. Bob was already helping him cope with missing his own dog, Jake.

Half an hour later, Carole plopped four cans of chunky dog food on the kitchen table. "There's a shop just around the corner."

"Thanks, Mom," said Neil distractedly. He had his head buried in a telephone book.

"What are you looking for?" she asked.

"A decent-sounding dog kennel," replied Neil.
"Here's one. Randall Farm Kennels. Great — they've
got a rescue center there, too. I'll call them right
away."

While Neil went into the living room to phone the
kennel, Sarah got down on her knees beside the
kitchen table and hugged the terrier to her. "Can't
we keep him?" she pleaded. "At least while we're
here?"

"I'm afraid we can't, honey," Carole said softly. "It's
not fair to let him become attached to us and then
leave him. He's a stray who needs a good home, and
the sooner we can get him to a rescue center, the better."

Neil came back a moment later. "That's that. I
spoke to Mr. Randall, who said he'd be happy to see
us tomorrow."

Carole nodded. "Good. We'll drop in at the kennel
on the way to Viola's house."

Neil ruffled the dog's furry head. He knew his parents were right. Boomerang Bob needed a proper
home. But as he lay in bed that night, with the Jack
Russell curled on the striped cotton rug by the bed,
he found himself wishing things could be different.

"Sorry, boy," he whispered. Bob twitched his ears
and lifted his head, staring at Neil with liquid brown
eyes. "You know I'd love to keep you as my dog, if

only we were staying here. But we're not. You're such a great little guy. We'll do our best to find you a good home. You need to belong to somebody."

Boomerang Bob gave a little yap, as though he completely agreed.

CHAPTER THREE

"**C**ome on, Bob," said Neil the following morning. "I'll take you for a run in the garden before we head out."

The Jack Russell terrier scampered past Neil through the kitchen door and into the garden.

As Neil stood on the doorstep watching the small white-and-tan dog sniffing around the bushes, he was thinking hard. Randall Farm Kennels wasn't that far away, so maybe he could still stop by every now and then to see Boomerang Bob. Before the vacation was over, he might even have been found a good home. He was such a friendly, happy little dog that surely any dog lover would want to adopt him.

Neil was just ushering Bob back inside when

someone rapped loudly at the front door and a woman's voice called out, "Anyone home?"

"Quick! Hide the dog!" hissed Carole.

Neil rushed back out into the garden with the terrier, hoping that they'd be camouflaged by the greenery and that Bob wouldn't bark.

A few tense minutes later, Emily came and found him. "It's OK, you can come in now. She's gone."

Neil followed her back inside and found his mother looking a little flustered.

"That was a close one!" she exclaimed. "It was the real estate agent. She popped in to see if everything was all right."

"And I noticed Boomerang Bob's food dish on the floor just in time and kicked it under the table," Emily added.

"Nice one, Em," said Neil.

"It just shows why we've got to get Bob out of here," Carole said. "It would be impossible to hide him for a whole week — and it wouldn't be fair to him, either."

"Or us," said Neil sadly, looking down at the smart little face of the dog he was growing so attached to.

Half an hour later, Bob Parker maneuvered the Land-cruiser off the Dingo Bay road and onto the main highway.

Neil sat in the front next to his father, with

Boomerang Bob fast asleep on the floor by his feet. Emily, Sarah, and Carole were fanning themselves with magazines in the backseat.

"I want to see a kangaroo," Sarah complained. "Mom said there are lots of them here."

"There are, Squirt," said Neil, who'd been reading up on them. "But you're not likely to see one by the sea. They live inland in packs called mobs, and each mob has its own territory."

"Don't worry," said Carole. "I expect we'll see some at the zoo."

"Next left!" Neil said suddenly. Neil had been given the map because he was a good navigator.

Bob Parker made the turn just in time.

"Now we've got to look out for a big green metal gate," Neil said.

"Is that it?" Emily pointed to some gates set into a wall just ahead of them.

Bob slowed down. "Let's see . . . Yes, Randall Farm Kennels. Here we are." He cut the engine and they all climbed out.

Carole rang the bell and was greeted by a chorus of barking dogs.

"Sounds just like home!" Neil laughed.

The gate was opened by a girl of about eleven, the same age as Neil. She had short blond hair and was wearing a purple T-shirt and cut-off jeans.

"G'day. I'm Jo Randall," she said, holding out her hand.

"Bob Parker. My son, Neil, called last night," Bob said.

"That's right. My dad told me," Jo replied. "The Parkers are here, Dad!" she called.

A tall, sun-reddened man with slicked-back blond hair came striding up and introduced himself as Jim Randall. He was soon deep in conversation with Bob and Carole.

"Where's the dog?" Jo asked Neil.

Boomerang Bob had disappeared into some tall grass. Neil hauled on his makeshift leash.

The Jack Russell pulled back. For a small dog, he was very strong. He was also very stubborn, and in the end Neil had to grab him and scoop him up into his arms.

"Naughty boy," he murmured affectionately. "This is our little stray," he said to Jo.

Her freckled forehead creased. "Why, that's Bob!" she exclaimed. She scratched the back of his head and the terrier gave a little whine of pleasure.

"How do you know his name?" Emily asked, surprised.

"Oh, because everybody knows Bob!"

"How come?" Neil inquired.

"He's the Dingo Bay beach dog. He showed up one day last summer and just hung around, I guess. Now everybody looks out for him and feeds him — especially the lifeguards."

"But he must belong to someone," said Emily.

"I wonder why no one came looking for him," added Neil.

Jo's face darkened. "This kind of thing happens quite a lot during the holiday season. People come and stay for a while — a few months, maybe — long enough to adopt a puppy. Then, when it's time to go home, they abandon it. It's awful!"

"Yes, it is," Neil agreed. "We run a rescue center and kennel in England. It's unbelievable how cruel some people can be, isn't it?"

"I can't imagine anyone being cruel to little Bob

here. He's so lovable." Jo let the dog nibble at her wrist. "You said you found him at the airport?"

Neil told Jo how the American girl had tried to smuggle him onto her plane.

Jo gave a derisive snort. "Stupid gal!" she scoffed. "I'll lend you a spare leash for him — I can see you're struggling with that one. Poor boy," she went on. "What a narrow escape. It's just as well he's been kept off the beach for a couple of days, though. They've got a surf carnival going on, and it's strictly no dogs on the sand. They're really sticking to the rules this year."

Jim Randall had overheard Jo, and he confirmed her words. "That's right. It's been particularly tough since Frank Fitzbrien took over as beach ranger. Dogs must be kept on a leash in all public places. Strays are definitely not allowed on the beaches or it's off to the dog pound!"

"What happens to them then?" Emily asked Mr. Randall.

"Oh, they try to find them homes. A lot of them end up here with us."

"Same as in England," said Emily.

Neil looked down the driveway, toward the kennel blocks. He was dying to see them and compare the facilities with those back home at King Street.

Jo followed his gaze. "Would you like a look-see?" she invited Neil and Emily.

"Definitely!" Neil grinned. "Come on, Em. Where's Squirt? She won't want to miss this."

Leaving their parents talking to Mr. Randall, the three young Parkers followed Jo into a large court-yard. A eucalyptus tree rattled its silvery leaves as the breeze struck it and provided welcome patches of shade. The kennels, which were ranged around the tree in a horseshoe shape, were similar in design to the ones at King Street.

"These are the rescue dogs," Jo explained. "They're all looking for new homes."

"Aw, look at this little puppy. Isn't he cute?" Sarah exclaimed, standing before a pen containing a young cocker spaniel with an appealing expression.

They heard a clang and turned to see a tall, thin boy of about nineteen, with blond hair like Jo's, who had been changing the water bowl in one of the pens. A woman came out of another pen holding a sack of dog biscuits.

"That's my brother Alan and my mom," said Jo, giving them a wave. They waved back, and Jo's mother came over to say hello before returning to finish the feeding.

Neil and Emily followed Jo down the row of pens. Inquisitive, hopeful, furry faces gazed at them from every pen. "You look pretty full," Neil remarked.

"Yes. We've just taken in a number of dogs that were rescued from a farm after their elderly owner died. It was very sad. There were about fifteen of them and they were all starving," Jo explained.

"Oh, that's awful! Are they all right now?" Emily asked anxiously.

"Well, the oldest dog had to be put down, but the rest are doing fine." Jo suddenly clicked her fingers. "Hey, Carly. Here, girl!"

A dog that had been dozing outside the house suddenly got to its feet and ran toward Jo, wagging its tail in greeting.

"What a great-looking dog," Neil said, admiring the powerfully muscled creature. Its gray coat was speckled with black, and its ears were perked up eagerly.

"Meet Carly — she's my special pet." Jo ruffled the dog's thick fur.

"What breed is she?" asked Neil. He'd never seen anything like her before.

"She's a Blue Heeler. Australian cattle dog is the correct name."

"She looks like she's got some collie in her," Neil said. "I've got a Border collie called Jake back home," he explained.

"You're right!" said Jo. "Australian cattle dogs were bred from the Scottish Blue Merle collie."

"Why are they called Blue Heelers?" asked Emily.

"Because they round up cattle by nipping at their heels," explained Jo. "They've got tons of energy and they can run for miles," she added, "so taking her for walks certainly keeps me fit. I feel safe with her, too. I know she's a match for anyone. Blue Heelers have even been known to fight roos."

"Do kangaroos attack dogs, then?" Sarah looked worried.

"Sometimes — if they think the dog's threatening them. Male roos in particular have a vicious kick. They can break a dog's back." Jo rubbed her pet's furry chest. "It's best to keep them apart."

They strolled around the boarding kennel next, meeting and greeting all the lodgers.

"King Street Kennels is really full at the moment, too," Neil informed Jo. "Lots of British people go away on vacation at this time of year."

"I wish I could visit your kennels." Jo sighed. "What a coincidence that you should come all the way from Pommy Land and end up here!"

"I wish we were here for longer. There's so much to see and do. But we've got eight days. School starts again soon." Neil grimaced.

"Tough luck! This is my summer vacation, so I've got another month off," Jo said with a grin. "Do you surf?"

"I've never had the chance to try," Neil admitted.

"Well, I'm pretty good at it. I could teach you," Jo offered. "Tell you what — I'll meet you down on the beach tomorrow afternoon. I'll help you take Bob back to the lifeguards, then I'll give you a lesson."

After Neil's parents had looked around the rescue center, Bob Parker announced that it was time to go.

"Mustn't be late for Viola or she'll start to worry and — hey, what's going on?" he exclaimed in surprise when he saw that Bob had started to follow Neil toward the car. "I thought he was staying here."

Neil shrugged sheepishly. "Sorry, Dad. It turns out that he's not really a stray after all. You see . . ."

Neil told his parents about Bob.

"Jo doesn't think it's fair to take him in when he's so well cared for by the lifeguards, so we're going to hand him back to them," Neil explained. "I hope it's OK, but I've told Jo I'll meet her on the beach at three o'clock tomorrow, which means we get to keep him till then."

Bob Parker frowned. "I'm not at all sure I agree with this." He turned to Jim Randall. "How do you feel about letting this dog loose on the beach again?"

Jim grinned. "As Neil explained to you, Bob's not really a stray. He's a bit like a communal pet. He's a tourist attraction, too. Vacationers get to know him and he just laps up all the pats and the affection, not to mention the sandwiches. Like Jo, I feel sure one of the lifeguards will adopt him. The whole team is really crazy about him."

"It'd be better if he could find a home with some-one he already knows," Emily said.

"Yes, it would," agreed Carole.

"Hmmm." Bob Parker grunted. "What's Viola go-ing to think when we drive up with a dog? How do we know he's going to get along with Sporty?"

"Bob gets along with everybody," Neil said. "And Jo's lent us a collar and leash, so he won't look like a stray."

"I suppose we'll have to hope for the best, then," said their father.

The Parkers said their farewells to the Randalls and climbed into the Land-cruiser.

Neil opened the window. "See you tomorrow!" he called to Jo as they drove off toward their next stop.

CHAPTER FOUR

Viola lived at Orchard Meadows, an idyllic-sounding spot about a hundred miles inland from Sydney.

As the Parkers' Land-cruiser drove up an avenue of trees to the top of a slope, Neil glimpsed a glittering expanse of water. "That must be Lake Barra," he said. "The road down to Victoria and Viola's house should be on our left."

They soon reached the turn. The narrow, winding road took them steeply down to the very edge of the lake.

"Isn't it beautiful?" Carole sighed as Bob stopped the car. "So this is what made Victoria turn her back on England."

"I can understand why," said Bob, gazing at the gleaming silvery water.

Neil looked at Viola's directions. "We follow that dirt road on our right."

They drove up the narrow road and soon the tires were crunching on gravel instead of dust, as Victoria and Viola's home rose up majestically in front of them.

"It's like an oasis!" cried Emily as she got out of the car and stood gazing at the lush greenery surrounding the house. The large white wooden house had a broad, tin-roofed veranda along the front of it that looked out over the lake.

"Hello, there!"

A short, stocky, silver-haired figure appeared on the porch and waved. It was Viola, great-aunt Victoria's friend.

No sign of a dog, thought Neil. *Where's Sporty?*

"Who's this little fellow, then?" Viola asked, pointing at the Jack Russell terrier. "Don't tell me you brought him all the way from England with you?" She laughed.

Once they had all introduced themselves and moved onto the large veranda for a round of deliciously chilled fresh orange juice, Neil explained to Viola how they had come upon Boomerang Bob.

"You can let him off the leash. He's quite safe here," Viola said.

The terrier was overjoyed to be allowed a run, and he promptly bounded to the edge of the lake, where he stood barking — apparently at nothing.

"Lively, little thing, isn't he?" Viola commented. "Sporty used to be like that when we first got him." She heaved a deep sigh.

I bet she's lonely out here on her own, thought Neil, then said, "Yes, Dad told us about Sporty. He's a Kelpie, isn't he? Where is he? I'd love to meet him."

"He's where he spends most of his time these days," Viola replied. She pushed her springy silver hair back off her perspiring forehead. Even though the veranda was shaded, the sun was beating down on its tin roof.

"What do you mean?" Carole asked gently.

"Come with me," said Viola. "The church-yard's just a short walk away."

Neil, Emily, and their father got up to follow her, but Carole said she'd stay behind with Sarah. The Jack Russell stayed behind, too. He'd drunk most of the bowl of water that Viola had given him and was now stretched out panting on a patch of lawn in the shade.

Viola moved very slowly, leaning on her stick. Emily walked close beside her, in case she needed a hand.

Several minutes later, they came to a small white church with a graveyard behind it. It was like any country cemetery back home, but the trees that over-hung the graves were different, the flowers that sprang from the grass seemed brighter, and the sky was so much bluer.

"Here we are," Viola said, leading them to a site at the foot of an acacia tree, "and here's Sporty."

The vivid scarlet flowers of a waratah bush growing next to the grave caught Neil's eye, and at first he couldn't see the dog. But as they got nearer, a patch of shadow detached itself from the base of the bush and developed two pointed ears and the saddest expression Neil had ever seen on the face of any dog.

"Here, Sporty," called Viola, delving into the pocket of her baggy blue trousers. She retrieved a dog chew and held it out to him. The Kelpie sniffed at the chew, then turned his head away. He was a black, medium-sized dog — about fifty inches high at the

shoulder, Neil estimated with his expert eye — but he looked thin and scrawny.

"Is he sick?" asked Emily.

"Nothing physical. He's been thoroughly checked," answered Viola.

"What is it, then?" wondered Neil.

Viola sighed. "He's been depressed ever since Victoria died," she explained. "The vet put him on some sort of pills for a while, but they made no difference. He seems to have lost his interest in life."

"But he's got you," Emily pointed out.

"Yes, I know, but it's not the same as far as Sporty is concerned. He adored Victoria, you see. I get along OK with him, but he always preferred her. Victoria had the magic touch as far as dogs were concerned."

"It's the Parker blood." Bob grinned.

"I think you're right," Viola replied.

"But you like dogs, don't you?" Neil had seen the way Viola had reacted to Boomerang Bob. She'd certainly seemed to take to him.

"Of course I like dogs! Who doesn't? But there was a special bond between Sporty and Victoria."

"Like me and Sam." It was Neil's turn to look sad for a moment, thinking of his beloved Border collie, Jake's dad, who had died from heart trouble.

"Victoria could never go anywhere without Sporty tagging along," Viola recalled. "You should have heard the howls if she left him behind! Kelpies need plenty of exercise. Victoria was still a great walker, even at eighty-two, and she was always taking Sporty for long hikes. I'm not much use to him because of my arthritic knees."

Neil crouched down beside the Kelpie. Although he knew the places where dogs loved to be stroked — around the ears, on the chest, beneath the chin — Sporty didn't react to his touch. In fact, the dog didn't seem to register that Neil was there at all. He appeared to be in a world of his own.

"How old is he?" Neil asked Viola.

"Let's see . . . he must be nearly nine. Getting on a bit, like me," Viola said.

Standing by Victoria's grave, they fell into a respectful silence for a few moments, broken only by the sound of Sporty panting.

"Come on, I'll take you home for a drink," said Viola. She took a leash out of her pocket and clipped it onto Sporty's collar. He followed her reluctantly, his muzzle and tail drooping.

As they reached the house again, a small dust cloud hurtled up to Neil and shook itself, covering him in cold droplets of water.

"Hey!" Neil shouted, brushing at his clothes. "I didn't ask for a shower!"

He heard Sarah giggling. "Bob's been swimming!" she shouted. "He nearly caught a fish!"

The Jack Russell danced several circles around the silent Kelpie. Then he darted up to Sporty, sniffed him, and shoved his nose forward. But the

Kelpie just swung his head away. Confused, the smaller dog barked at him. Sporty simply ignored him. He even ignored Carole, who spoke soothingly to him and reached out to stroke him.

"This dog definitely needs help," she said when Neil told her where they'd found him. "Have you thought about taking him to a dog psychologist?"

Viola gave a dismissive laugh. "You must be joking!" she said. "You might find such newfangled things in the city, but not hereabouts." She turned to Bob. "Why don't you all take a walk by the lake and watch the sunset while I prepare our dinner?"

Viola went into the house and returned with a plastic tube. "Better slap some of this on," she said. "The bugs come out around this time and they'd probably relish some nice fresh blood!" Viola took hold of Sporty's collar. "I'll take Sporty in with me, otherwise he'll go sulking off to the churchyard again."

"Poor Sporty." Emily sighed.

"I'm *sure* something could be done for him," Neil said. "I've never come across a dog yet who couldn't be helped in some way."

"I'll try to think of something, too," Emily promised.

After their lakeside walk, they ate dinner on the veranda. Viola had produced a simple but wonderful meal of fresh grilled fish and salad, followed by fruit and ice cream. Boomerang Bob begged for scraps, but Sporty ignored the whole proceedings. When Viola put his dinner in front of him, the Kelpie nosed at it for a while, then walked indoors and flopped down in the hall. Neil was really worried about him.

After Sarah was put to bed, Bob and Carole started reminiscing with Viola about family history. A chilly breeze was blowing off the lake. The adults went indoors, but Neil and Emily put sweatshirts on and stayed out on the veranda with glasses of Viola's homemade lemonade and a second helping of ice cream.

Emily yawned. "I'm tired."

Neil smiled. "Me, too. Let's turn in. Where's Boomerang Bob?"

"I don't know. Isn't he under your chair?" Emily asked lazily. "He usually is."

"No," said Neil. "Let's go and find him."

They wandered around the garden but couldn't spot the little dog.

"Maybe he went inside," said Emily.

Sporty was no longer lying in the hall. When they reached the kitchen, they found the Kelpie by the back door, fast asleep on the doormat. The Jack Russell was dozing beneath the table.

"Let's leave them here for the night — they seem to be getting along all right," Viola said, coming out from the living room.

"I'll just refill their water bowls, then," said Neil. He'd been hoping that Bob would spend his last night of freedom with him. He called to the terrier, who cocked one tan ear but didn't stir.

"OK," Neil said, "have it your way. I'll leave my bedroom door open in case you change your mind."

Neil found it hard to get to sleep that night. It was so hot and sticky that he was almost glad he didn't have a warm dog anywhere near him. Strange night-time noises drifted in through the mosquito mesh fitted to the open window.

He sighed and turned over. Then, before he knew it, a noise broke through his dreams and woke him. It was getting light and he glanced at his watch. Quarter to six!

He jumped as something moved nearby.

"Neil? Are you awake? What was that noise?" said Emily.

"I don't know," he replied sleepily. "Let's go and investigate. Maybe a possum got into the house."

Making sure they didn't disturb Sarah, they pulled on some clothes and then crept quietly downstairs. The sounds were coming from the kitchen. The door was slightly open and Neil put an eye to the crack. "Em! Quick! You've got to see this. It's the dogs!" he whispered.

Emily crouched in front of Neil and they both watched Boomerang Bob running around in circles, snapping at his stubby tail, stumbling into chairs and table legs. He really was acting like a clown. And watching him, panting eagerly with his head to one side, was Sporty.

All at once, as if aware that he'd caught the older dog's attention, the little Jack Russell ceased his solo game and started to play with the Kelpie's tail instead — bounding up and swiping at it with his paw, running away, then bouncing back to give it a little nip.

Sporty sat stock-still — it seemed as though he could hardly believe that the madcap youngster was teasing him.

Every time the terrier swiped Sporty's tail, the Kelpie would jerk it out of the way. Bob crouched, growled, then launched another attack, and each time he did so, Sporty looked more interested.

Then something amazing happened. Sporty suddenly joined in, and the two of them ran all over the kitchen in a crazy game of chase.

Emily laughed out loud. The back door opened abruptly and there was Viola, framed in the doorway. "Why are you two up so early?" she inquired.

Then she spotted the dogs and her hand flew to her mouth. "Oh, well, I never! Would you believe it?" she declared. "Sporty looks like a puppy again."

Boomerang Bob chose that moment to skid into her and head-butt her ankle. "Shoo, the pair of you, shoo! Out into the garden with you," she scolded playfully.

Sporty trotted across the step, then looked back over his shoulder to make sure Bob was following. The two went scampering down the path and into the bushes, snarling and yapping as they ran.

"Wasn't that great?" said Emily.

Viola laughed.

"Success!" cried Neil.

CHAPTER FIVE

An hour later, as everyone was digging into fresh fruit salad for breakfast, Boomerang Bob and Sporty were already sitting side by side on the kitchen step, just like old friends.

"Isn't it great?" said Neil to Viola. "Sporty's really livened up since Bob came."

"I'm so glad you brought him!" she declared. "I never thought I'd see Sporty show any interest in anything again."

"You should have seen the two of them earlier on, Mom!" exclaimed Emily. She described the scene she and Neil had witnessed that morning.

"Bob certainly seems to be doing Sporty some good!" Carole laughed.

Viola smiled fondly at the two dogs. "Sporty's eaten the biggest breakfast he's had in months."

"Maybe all he needed was another dog to keep him company and stop him missing Victoria so much," said Neil. Then a marvelous idea occurred to him. "Hey — why don't you keep Boomerang Bob, Viola? He needs a good home."

To Neil it seemed the obvious thing to do, but Viola began shaking her head. "He's a terrific little dog, Neil, but I'm afraid he's far too young and lively for me. He'd need lots of exercise, and I just couldn't supply it."

"But he's got your big garden to run around in," Neil pointed out. He couldn't believe Viola wouldn't take Bob, not when he'd had such a good effect on Sporty.

Viola shook her head again. "He's too young and active. I couldn't look after him properly at my age. He'd get under my feet, and I'd trip over him."

Although Neil knew that the Jack Russell needed a lot of walking, which would be hard for Viola to manage with her arthritis, he couldn't help but feel disappointed. However, Viola was adamant, and that, it seemed, was that.

It was just after eleven o'clock when they waved good-bye to Viola.

Neil's heart was heavy. Later that day he would

have to meet Jo and hand Boomerang Bob over to the lifeguards. Things would have been perfect if the terrier could have found a permanent home with Viola and Sporty.

"Some old people don't like change," Carole remarked as the Land-cruiser began the climb up to the ridge that led them out of the picturesque valley.

"And Viola's right — Bob would be a real handful for her with her arthritis," Bob Parker added.

"But they loved each other!" exclaimed Sarah.

"Yes, Bob and Sporty did seem to take a liking to each other. But it can't be helped," her father said. "Anyway, Boomerang Bob will be boomeranging back to the beach he came from and the people he knows. He should be happy there."

Neil looked gloomy. "Jo told me that all dogs in the Sydney area had to be registered and wear an identity tag with their registration details on it. If someone notices Bob's not wearing one, they may give him to the authorities."

"In which case he'll probably end up back with your friend Jo again," Bob Parker pointed out. "That can't be a bad thing, can it? So don't worry, OK?"

"OK," replied Neil reluctantly.

But Neil *was* worried. Viola could have given Boomerang Bob the ideal home and stopped him leading a beachcomber life. And what about Sporty? With nothing to lift him out of his depression, would the

Kelpie simply pine away? Neil's thoughts dwelled on the two dogs for the rest of their journey back to Sydney.

They took the long route, stopping frequently to admire the views, and arrived at their bungalow early that afternoon.

"Perfect timing," commented Carole, glancing at her watch as she climbed out of the car. "It's not good to be out in the hot sun between twelve and three, but by the time we've had lunch — Hey, slow down!"

Carole stepped aside quickly as Boomerang Bob leaped out of the car and began barking and sniffing at the flowers bordering the bungalow's front lawn.

Neil jumped out after him.

"Get him inside, Neil," said Carole. "We don't want to attract attention, remember?"

But just at that moment, a motorbike roared up beside them and braked suddenly.

The driver — a fair-haired, tanned young man — removed his helmet and looked straight at the Jack Russell terrier frolicking on the grass. His brow creased in a slight frown.

"Oops," muttered Neil, "too late."

"Hey, that's Bob!" the man called to his passenger — another tanned young man in brightly colored shorts and a T-shirt.

"Yeah — that's *our* dog!" said the passenger. "What

are you doing with him? You'd better hand him over before we report you for stealing him!"

"We *didn't* steal him!" Neil yelled indignantly.

The bikers dismounted and the driver propped up his bike.

"He's been missing for four days now," said the passenger. "We were worried that he might have gotten himself run over."

"Who are you?" Bob asked the bikers.

The tanned young men introduced themselves as Brett and Leo, members of the Dingo Bay Lifesaving Club.

"We're in the middle of the surf carnival contests on the beach and our team's been losing heavily," said Brett. "We think it's because we lost our mascot here."

"He's your mascot?" asked Emily.

"He sure is, and now that he's back we might start winning! Come on, little fella . . ." Brett scooped Bob out of Neil's arms. The terrier obviously recognized him because he whined and licked Brett's chin. Brett took a few steps backward, laughing and holding Boomerang Bob away from his face.

"Let me explain what really happened, so you won't think it was us who stole him," said Neil firmly.

"Yes," said Emily. "We were actually just on our way to give him back to you."

When Neil finished telling his story, Brett and Leo were quick to apologize.

"That's cool," said Leo. "Thanks for looking after him."

"Yeah," echoed Brett. "But we gotta run, mate. We're competing in a surf-ski race soon. We can't take Bob with us on the bike, so we'll trust you to bring him down to us at the rescue hut — OK?" Brett handed Bob back to Neil. "I'm sure our luck'll change once we've got him back."

"Make sure you cheer for the Dingoes!" added Leo.

"We will," promised Emily.

*   *   *

"This is bliss!" said Carole, wiggling her bare toes in the warm sand on Dingo Bay Beach. She lay on her back, beaming at the blue sky.

There were lots of family groups dotted along the length of sand, and a large cluster of people farther to the right, around the rescue hut where the events were being held. Way out to sea, several white-sailed dinghies were cruising slowly along the horizon.

Emily had stripped down to her swimsuit, and her mother was plastering her back with sunscreen lotion. "You're next, Neil," she said. "You know how dangerous the sun is. Make sure you've got plenty of cream on before you go to meet Jo."

The peace and quiet of the beach was shattered by a booming loudspeaker announcing the next surf carnival event.

"We'd better get over there," said Neil, consulting his waterproof sports watch. "C'mon, Dad. The Dingoes will be on soon. We'll watch the surf-ski race."

"I'll see you later," said Carole. "I'm going to stay here and soak up the sun. I think Sarah would be better off staying near me, in the shade of the beach umbrella. The sun's too strong for her sensitive skin."

"I'd better give Boomerang Bob some water before I take him, then," Neil said. "And I'll keep him hidden as much as I can."

Sarah's face started to crumple. He knew how she

felt. He was going to miss the perky little Jack Russell, too.

Neil waited for the terrier to finish drinking then scooped him up from the sand and wrapped him in a towel. "Come on, boy. Time to take you home," he said, rubbing his face against the small dog's wiry fur.

Emily and Bob Parker found a good spot from which to watch the events. Neil made a mental note of where they were, then went to look for Jo. He tried not to draw attention to himself as he walked toward the rescue hut with Boomerang Bob in his arms.

He found Jo sitting on the low wall that separated the beach from the road.

"Hi, Neil, Hi, Bob!"

The dog placed a front paw on Jo's arm while she scratched him beneath the chin.

"I just saw Brett," she said. "He asked where you and Bob were."

"Where is he?" asked Neil.

"Over there, behind the lookout post," said Jo. The tall wooden chair, which was always manned by a lifeguard in the daytime, was about four yards in front of the rescue hut — surrounded by a throng of spectators.

"Right. Let's go!" With Boomerang Bob clutched tightly in his arms, Neil ducked under the red rope that cordoned off the competitors' area.

They peered through the crowds and did their best to catch Brett's eye, but he had his back turned to them and was fiddling with the starter motor of an inflatable rescue boat.

Suddenly, a short, dark, wiry man of about forty strode up to them, smiling as he caught sight of Boomerang Bob. "Nice to see you again, cobber! We thought you were shark food for a while there," he said, reaching out to pat the little dog.

"Hi," said Neil. "Do you know Bob?"

"Sure do. I'm Harry — head lifeguard around here."

"Great," said Jo. "Then can you get Bob to Brett and Leo?"

The lifeguard shook his head. "Sorry, mate. No can do. Not with Frank Fitzbrien here, judging the events. If he saw Bob, he'd make us take him straight to the dog pound. You'll have to bring Bob back after Frank leaves."

"But Brett and Leo need him now," Jo insisted.

"I gave them my word I'd bring him," Neil added anxiously. He shot a desperate look across the sand. The loudspeaker was booming again, and several lifesaving teams, all wearing multicolored club caps, were lining up on the sand. He felt sure he recognized Leo and Brett among them.

"Sorry. If it were up to me . . ." Harry shrugged apologetically. "Unfortunately, it's not. I'll tell them you came. Now, I really must get back to my duties. Make sure you keep Bob well hidden."

Harry strode off toward the competition area. Jo and Neil looked at each other.

"Now what are we going to do?" Jo asked.

CHAPTER SIX

As soon as Sarah saw Neil trudging across the sand toward her with Boomerang Bob in his arms, her face lighted up with pleasure. "You've still got him! Yippee!"

Emily laughed. "No wonder the Dingoes were last in the surf-ski race," she said, giving the dog an affectionate pat.

Neil told Sarah and Carole what had happened. "Jo's gone home. I'm going to meet up with her again tomorrow to do some surfing."

"Right. So we'll do what the head lifeguard suggested and try again later," said Carole reassuringly.

Neil nodded, gave the dog some water, and settled down on a towel in the shade to spend the rest of the afternoon reading a book.

*   *   *

In the evening, just before dinner, the entire Parker family walked along the bay toward the lifeguards' rescue hut, intending to leave Bob there before going out to eat. As they drew near the hut, it was clear that it was locked and deserted.

A passer-by told Neil that the lifeguards had packed up and gone about half an hour ago. Neil pretended to be disappointed, but he was secretly feeling pretty pleased. This meant he would have Boomerang Bob to himself for at least one more night!

Neil's father sighed. "We'll just have to take Bob with us to the restaurant. We'll all sit at a fancy table inside, and you can sit outside with him, Neil," he joked.

"Suits me!" Neil grinned.

They walked back along the beach and, as it turned out, there happened to be a large table free outside, so they were all able to sit with the Jack Russell.

While Neil ate, he listened to the general family chatter and then, finishing his food, leaned back in his chair. The Jack Russell nuzzled his foot underneath the table.

I'd be very happy with this as a permanent way of life — sunshine, beaches, restaurants, and Boomerang Bob, thought Neil. *If it wasn't for Jake back in freezing cold Compton, I'd be seriously tempted!*

"I'm going to get up early tomorrow and take Bob down to the rescue hut before any of the race officials get there," Neil suggested.

"Good idea," Carole said. "We promised Sarah we'd take her to the zoo tomorrow afternoon."

"Yippee!" cried Sarah.

"And I'm sure they don't allow dogs in the zoo," finished Carole.

"We've got a lot more sightseeing to do in Sydney, you know," said Bob Parker. "They won't allow dogs in the shops and museums, either."

"Calm down, calm down!" exclaimed Neil. "I'm sure nothing else can go wrong. And if it does, then we'll let the Randalls take him in. I want the best for him, too," he said passionately.

Despite this hiccup in getting Bob back to his lifeguard friends, Neil was in a great mood. There were still six days left in their vacation, he still had Boomerang Bob, and he also had the promise of a surfing lesson from Jo the following day. Life was looking good!

"Can you believe it'll be New Year's Eve tomorrow?" Carole announced the next morning at breakfast. "How are we going to celebrate?"

They were all busily discussing it when someone rapped at the door. As usual, Neil rushed Boomerang Bob out to hide him in the bushiest part of the garden.

The unexpected visitors were Jo and her dad.

"I'm on my way to pick up supplies for the kennel, so I thought I'd drop my daughter off," Jim Randall said.

"Hello, Mr. Randall," said Neil, coming back into the kitchen.

"Hi, Neil. Jo told me what happened yesterday. Frank Fitzbrien's influence is getting a bit out of hand, in my opinion. It's probably because he's new on the job."

"It's terrible," agreed Jo. "Right now, someone's only got to let their dog off the leash for a second to expect an instant ticket."

"Perhaps he's got a grudge against dogs," Neil suggested.

"He probably prefers sharks," joked Emily.

"Come on, Jo," said Neil, "it's nearly nine! We've got to get the Dingoes mascot to them today or they'll never forgive us. Coming, Em?"

"No — I haven't finished my breakfast. See you later, OK?" his sister replied. Neil had a strong feeling that the real reason Emily wasn't coming was because she couldn't face having to say good-bye to Boomerang Bob.

"I hope you've still got space in your rescue center, Jim, in case they can't give Bob back today," Carole Parker said anxiously.

"Always room for a bonzer little tyke like him," Mr. Randall said cheerfully, patting the terrier as he leaped up and down in front of him.

* * *

A few minutes later, Neil and Jo were walking along the pavement toward the lifeguards' rescue hut.

"He's walking very well to heel," said Jo, looking down at Bob. "I bet he'd be easy to train. He's naturally quite well-behaved."

"I think you spoke too soon," Neil said, laughing as the Jack Russell seized one of Jo's sneaker laces in his teeth and tugged it, almost pulling her over.

They had nearly reached the hut when Brett came roaring up alongside on his motorbike. "G'day!" he called cheerfully. "So you've brought our mascot back at last. We could have used him yesterday. We lost two events."

"We did try," pleaded Jo.

"Yeah, I know. Harry told us. He's our boss. Leo and I are just volunteers doing lifesaving part-time. Harry's a professional, though — he trains people like us," explained Brett. The lifeguard took a good look around. "Better be quick. I don't know what time Fitzbrien will get here," he said ominously.

"He's probably up in town, following some poor old lady who's let her Yorkie off the leash for two seconds," said Jo.

Brett grinned. "I bet you're right!"

"I don't see why you can't adopt Bob properly," Neil said.

Brett shrugged regretfully. "I'd love to. Trouble is, I'm in a house-share with Leo and some of the other lifeguards, and our landlady won't let us have pets. And anyway, we're all off to out-of-state universities after the summer. That's why we've been keeping him at the rescue hut."

Brett crouched down and rubbed the terrier's ears. "You like it there, don't you, boy? There's a fan and it's nice and cool. It's like a big dog kennel. We keep lots of your favorite tidbits here, too, don't we?"

Neil laughed as Brett rubbed noses with the Jack Russell. They were obviously great friends. It was a pity about Brett's landlady.

"OK, I'll take him now," said Brett. But no sooner had he taken hold of Bob's leash, than the Jack Russell spotted a lizard scurrying across the sand. The

leash slipped from Brett's hand and Bob sped off in pursuit, ignoring cries of "Come back, you little tyke!"

Neil, Jo, and Brett charged after Bob, but every time they called his name, he glanced around playfully and kept on running. He was really enjoying himself.

"No dogs on the beach! Who's in charge of that animal?" boomed a voice nearby.

"Oops," hissed Jo. "It's Frank the Tank!"

Neil and Jo froze as a big man in a short-sleeved white shirt and khaki shorts climbed out of a patrol car and strode toward them. He was deeply tanned and stood well over six feet tall, with thick black curly hair cut very short. His massive shoulders and biceps bulged out of his shirt and the top buttons were open, showing a thick dark mat of wiry chest hair. Neil could see how he'd earned his nickname, Frank the Tank!

"G'day, Mr. Fitzbrien," said Brett, confirming the big man's identity.

The beach ranger gave the young lifeguard a curt nod and continued to scowl at Neil.

"*Well?*" he thundered. "Does that dog belong to you?"

"Um, yes!" replied Neil.

Jo gasped.

Boomerang Bob chose that moment to come trotting up as fast as his short legs could carry him. He walked up to Neil and sat on his foot, as if backing up Neil's claim.

Frank Fitzbrien bent down and examined the Jack Russell's collar. "Is this your collar?" he asked sternly. "It should have a tag with the dog's details on it."

"He — he lost it yesterday and we haven't had time to get another one yet," Neil said impulsively.

"Hmmm. What's your name and address?" demanded the ranger.

Neil couldn't remember the number of the bungalow, so he made one up. Brett supplied the name of the street.

"I'll check the records," Frank Fitzbrien threatened. "Now, don't let me see this dog running loose around here again. It's my job to keep this beach free from troublesome mutts like yours." He turned on his heels and walked back toward his patrol car.

Brett was stunned. "Frank strikes again!"

"Why did you tell him Bob was yours, Neil?" asked Jo.

"Because otherwise he would have taken Bob away," replied Neil.

The terrier, who was lying at Neil's feet, pricked an ear at the sound of his name. The other ear was folded down, giving him a lopsided look that was accentuated by the tan patch over his left eye.

"I suppose you'd better hang on to him for a while longer, Neil," said Brett. "Maybe you can sneak him past Frank later on — or tomorrow."

"I'll try," sighed Neil. "But I'm not looking forward to going back to the bungalow with Boomerang Bob. Dad's going to kill me!"

Jo and Brett laughed. "Good luck!" they chorused.

"What would you have done, Mom?" pleaded Neil, looking at his mother for support.

"I probably would have done exactly the same thing you did," Carole Parker admitted. "Your dad's just mad because having a dog with us is making our day more difficult."

Neil's parents were leaving him and the terrier at a café in a park near Sydney's Taronga Zoo. They had asked the waitress to keep an eye on the two of them. They couldn't risk any more incidents involving Neil, dogs, and the law!

Neil, however, thought that spending a few more hours with Bob would easily compensate for missing out on the trip to the zoo.

It was two and a half hours before his family returned. The time had passed quite quickly for Neil, since he'd taken Bob for a long walk around the park, keeping him firmly on the leash.

Sarah was thrilled to bits from having had a close encounter with a koala, while Emily couldn't stop talking about a duck-billed platypus.

"Has Bob been good while we were away?" asked Carole.

"No — he stole my ice cream," Neil grumbled. "I

put it down on the bench while I fastened my shoe-laces and the next moment it was gone."

Everyone burst out laughing.

"Never mind. I'll buy you another. In fact, let's all have one," offered Bob Parker. Neil knew that he'd been forgiven — for now, at least.

Back at the bungalow that evening, Bob Parker called Viola. When he got off the phone, he looked troubled.

"What's wrong?" Neil asked anxiously.

"It's poor old Sporty. It seems that he stopped eating again after we left. Viola had to take him to the vet.

"Is he OK?" asked Emily.

"They've given him something to stimulate his appetite, but Viola says it doesn't seem to be working. He's getting thinner and weaker by the day."

"But he was eating so well while we were there," Carole pointed out.

"You know why that was," Neil reminded her. "It was because he had a friend."

"Maybe," Bob said. "It's a pity . . ."

It was the greatest pity ever, in Neil's opinion.

"I also called the Randalls," Bob went on. He paused, and Neil held his breath. "Apparently, a local family went on vacation and left their dogs behind, locked in a shed."

"How can people *do* things like that?" said Emily emotionally.

"They don't *deserve* to have dogs," Neil said furiously. "What happened?"

"They'd left dry food and water out for them," continued Bob, "but neighbors heard the dogs barking and called the police. So the Randalls have taken in the dogs."

"Does that mean there's no room for Bob?" Neil asked.

"Not for the moment, no," his father replied.

Neil couldn't believe it. He'd won another reprieve! It was down to him now to get Boomerang Bob fixed up with a home. Though he only had five days to do it, he was determined to find the lovable, spirited Jack Russell the best owner possible. He deserved it.

CHAPTER SEVEN

"**W**ow, just look at those teeth! That thing's worse than the one in *Jaws*!" Neil exclaimed as a huge shark reared its ugly head out of the water. It was shark-feeding time at Oceanworld in Manly Cove.

Emily gave a frightened shudder. "It might bite that man's hand off!" she said anxiously.

Neil laughed. "Don't worry, Em — the people feeding them are experts. They know what they're doing."

They blinked as they walked out into the dazzling sunshine where their mother was waiting with Sarah.

"Haven't they got a Hamsterworld?" Sarah asked hopefully. She was missing Fudge, her pet hamster.

Everyone laughed.

At that moment, Bob Parker returned from a long walk with Boomerang Bob, and they all set off toward the patio of a nearby beachfront café for lunch.

Boomerang Bob settled under Neil's chair, snuggling against his leg.

While they were deciding what to order, someone called, "Hi, Neil!" They looked around to see Harry, the head lifeguard, approaching them.

Neil introduced Harry to the rest of the Parker family.

"I'm glad I ran into you," Harry said. "The lifeguards are having a New Year's Eve barbecue and a few fireworks on the beach tonight, to raise money for charity. Would you all like to come?"

"Yes, please!" chorused Emily and Sarah.

"I think that means we'll be there." Carole laughed.

Harry smiled, but then took a quick glance around. "No sign of Frank the Tank. Good. Here, let me take Bob, will you? The Dingoes are desperate to win at least one event today."

"Will he be OK?" asked Neil.

"Don't worry, he'll be well hidden. I'll take him back to my place when I finish work tonight — so he won't be scared by the fireworks. I figure my wife can cope with him for one night."

"Good thinking," said Bob Parker.

"Have you got any dogs of your own?" Neil asked

Harry, hoping there might be a chance of Harry offering Bob a home.

"Three," the head lifeguard replied. "My wife's got two spaniels, Lucy and Lola, and there's Plug, my boxer. They're all very friendly and get along with other dogs, so I'm sure there'll be no trouble when I bring Bob home."

He paused. Neil held his breath. Then he heard what he'd been hoping for. "I'm actually wondering if I should adopt Bob. I know we've got three dogs already, but as far as I'm concerned, it's the more the merrier. My youngest boy would love a dog of his own, and I think this little guy would be perfect."

"It would be great if you could," Neil said, voicing everyone's thoughts.

Harry smiled. "I'll ask my wife. See you later!" The head lifeguard walked off with Boomerang Bob trotting beside him.

It happened so quickly that Neil hardly knew what had hit him. One minute, the lively Jack Russell had been there with them, and the next, he was gone.

Bob Parker looked at the crestfallen faces around the table. "Cheer up! All's well that ends well, right? It looks as if Bob might have found a home after all."

"I've got a good feeling about Harry. I'm sure he's great with dogs," said Neil. Then he sighed deeply as he watched Harry and Boomerang Bob disappearing into the distance.

After lunch, everyone went back to the bungalow to get their beach things. The house seemed quiet and empty without the energetic Jack Russell bounding around. Neil looked sadly at the water bowl and feeding dish they'd put down for Bob that morning, and he sighed again as he washed them up and put them away.

Neil knew he'd miss Boomerang Bob like crazy for the rest of his vacation. But missing him was worth it if the friendly little dog found a good home with Harry and his family. If Viola wouldn't have him, then Harry was an excellent second choice.

Half an hour later, as everyone picked their way through the vacationers on Dingo Bay Beach, Neil spotted Jo in a vivid purple swimsuit sitting on the sand near the spot where the Parkers usually pitched their beach umbrella. She was with her older brother, Alan, who had given her a lift with the boogie boards.

Neil took off his white baseball cap with the words *King Street Kennels* embroidered in green. "If Jo's going to teach me to surf," he explained, "I don't want to lose it in the water."

Minutes later, Neil had left his family sunbathing and was wading out into the waves. The tide was coming in, but there was no breeze and the surf

wasn't too high. The conditions were ideal for a beginner surfer.

Jo showed Neil how to bodysurf by pushing the boogie board onto the crest of a wave, throwing yourself flat on it, and letting the wave roll you to shore. It was a lot of fun, and Neil fell off several times before he got the hang of it. At one point, he even managed to balance upright on the board just long enough for Jo to take a quick photograph of him to show his friends back home.

They had just gotten out of the water when they heard the loudspeaker announcing that the afternoon's surf carnival events were about to begin. First on the agenda was a race along the shore. As if running on sand wasn't difficult enough, the lifeguards also had to carry a surfboard under their arm!

"Let's go," Neil said, and the pair dashed across the sand to the roped-off enclosure where the contests were held.

Brett spotted them and gave the thumbs-up sign. "Hi!" he shouted.

"Good luck!" Neil replied.

"Thanks, mate! I think we'll do OK now that we've got our lucky mascot," Brett said with a mischievous wink.

Jo nudged Neil, "Look," she said, and pointed at Harry, the head lifeguard. He was wearing a very baggy navy parka that looked suspiciously bulky. As Neil stared at it, he saw a movement, then the flash of a pink tongue beneath a black nose.

He grinned. "Good thing Bob isn't a Rottweiler!" he joked. "Harry's taking a huge risk, though. If Frank the Tank sees him . . ."

"Yes — Harry would be in a lot of trouble for deliberately breaking rules," Jo added, picking up on Neil's line of thought.

At that moment, however, Frank Fitzbrien had little chance of spotting one small, well-hidden dog. The beach ranger was seated on a wooden platform shaded by a canvas awning, busily writing notes about each team. He was taking his job as a competition judge every bit as seriously as his job upholding local bylaws.

Jo and Neil, who had now been joined by the rest of the Parkers, cheered like crazy when Brett and Leo's team won the running race.

The next event was announced as an "R and R competition."

"It stands for Rescue and Resuscitation," Jo explained. "Someone pretends they're drowning, and the teams have to go out on a paddle-board and rescue them, then bring them back to shore and pretend to revive them. You'll see soon."

"And Nigel's lost it! He's off his board!" shouted the enthusiastic announcer. "The teams are in the surf. Dave from the Red Rock team is first to reach him. Oh, no — Dave's fallen off, too! But Leo's there — Leo from our Dingoes team, folks! And Leo's bringing Nigel back to shore."

"Hey, this is so exciting!" cried Emily.

"Sure is," agreed Neil. "Boomerang Bob is really having an effect!"

"Yes, he's got him!" continued the announcer. "And Jilly from the Dingoes is helping to resuscitate Nigel. She's putting him into the recovery position. Yes, Nigel's OK, he's sitting up. Well done, Dingoes!"

The Parkers and Jo shouted and cheered along with the rest of the audience.

"Bob's brought their good luck back, hasn't he?" said Sarah, grinning.

Neil and Jo exchanged happy smiles.

Just after seven that night, a very hungry Neil and his family set out for the lifeguards' barbecue. There were loads of people on the beach, all in a celebratory mood. A group of musicians were playing a mixture of Aboriginal and contemporary music. When they took a break, pop music was played over a PA system.

The food was great — barbecued sausages, steaks, and fish, with bowls of rice and salad set out on tables in the sand. Neil and Emily sat chattering for most of the evening, while their parents danced almost nonstop until midnight.

Suddenly, there was a loud *whoosh!* as a brilliant rocket shot into the sky over the ocean and sprinkled the water with green and gold stars.

It was New Year's Day!

For the next twenty minutes, the sky was aglow with fiery patterns and exploding colors. The band played "Auld Lang Syne," and everyone joined hands and sang and wished one another a happy New Year.

"I hate to say this, Neil," said Carole Parker the following afternoon, as they drove back after a day out in Sydney, "but sightseeing is much easier without a terrier in tow."

"That's if you want to do things like shopping. I'd rather be walking a dog!" grumbled Neil.

On his lap, Neil clutched his only purchase of the day — a squeaky rubber shark from Paddy's Market, a huge market in central Sydney that seemed to sell almost everything. It was the perfect doggy gift to take back home to his Border collie, Jake.

As Bob Parker neared the bungalow, he was irritated to see that another driver had taken his usual parking spot right outside the house. Muttering angrily, he pulled in behind it.

The driver's door of the dusty car opened and a man got out — a very apologetic-looking man, holding a small, wriggling, tan-and-white dog.

"Oh, good!" said Neil.

"Oh, no!" groaned his father.

"Sorry," apologized Harry, "but I'm afraid I'm going to have to ask you if you can look after Boomerang Bob again."

"No problem!" said Neil cheerfully, relieving the head lifeguard of his wriggling burden. He tickled the little dog under his chin, then set him down on the floor.

The Jack Russell promptly barged into Emily's leg. She laughed and patted him. "What happened?" she asked Harry. "I thought you said Bob would be OK at the rescue hut?"

"I thought he would be," admitted Harry, "but

Frank spotted Brett giving Bob some water in the doorway. That man's got X-ray vision! He wanted to take Bob straight to the dog pound, but luckily Brett pretended that he'd run away while I managed to smuggle him out."

"Why can't you take him home with you again?" Neil asked Harry. "I thought you were going to adopt him."

Harry's face fell. "I really wanted to, but my wife said no. She says that four kids, three dogs, two cats, and a rabbit is a big enough menagerie for her to manage. It's not that she doesn't like Bob. She just says we've got enough mouths to feed already, and one more, even a small one, is just too much."

"Poor old Bob. So you're homeless again," Neil said sympathetically, patting the Jack Russell. The dog gazed up at him adoringly.

Harry hadn't missed the affection between the small terrier and Neil. "I thought bringing him back to you was the best thing to do, while we all try to think of a solution," he said.

Neil began to lose his cool. "Surely there must be someone!" he exploded. "Australia's supposed to be a land of dog lovers!"

"It is," agreed Harry. "It's just bad timing, that's all. It's the holiday season and lots of people are away. Boarding kennels are overflowing with dogs, and nobody even wants to think about taking on a pet until life settles down again. He's such a great dog that I'm sure someone will take him eventually."

"Eventually is no good. We fly home on the fourth," said Neil glumly. "That means we're only here for another three days!"

"It's such a bummer," added Emily.

"The Dingo Bay Surf Carnival finishes tomorrow," said Harry. "I think Bob will be OK on the beach after that because Frank won't be around so much. And if it's still a problem, then maybe I can persuade my wife to have him for a few days, just until there's room again at the Randalls' rescue center."

Neil's heart was heavy. It seemed that nothing was working out for the lovable little dog. He'd boomeranged back to them again. Who knew what fate would befall him after they'd gone back to Compton?

Neil sighed deeply as he looked into Bob's bright, hopeful eyes. "It's really sad," he told Harry. "We've got the perfect home for him, except that Viola doesn't think she could manage him. You see, she can't walk very well . . ."

Neil told Harry all about Viola and Sporty.

When he'd finished, Harry said, "What a shame." He looked thoughtful, but then added, "I'm sure we'll find somewhere for him somehow. I'd best be off now — see you later."

After the head lifeguard had gone, Neil crouched down and fondled Boomerang Bob's ears. "It's great to have you back," he said. "I really don't know what we're going to do with you, though. I've never known such a small dog to be such a big problem!"

CHAPTER EIGHT

"**C**ome on, Bob, let's take you out for a walk, OK?" said Neil early that evening, taking the Jack Russell's leash off the hook on the back door.

"Can I come, too?" asked Emily. "I could use a walk myself. I miss exercising the dogs at King Street."

"I'll give you a lift," volunteered their dad.

Harry had tipped them off to a quiet, secluded beach where they could get away with letting Bob off the leash for a run.

It was quite difficult to find, at the bottom of a winding lane that turned out to be too narrow and steep for the large Land-cruiser. Bob Parker left the car at the top of the cliff and they walked the rest of the way down, with Boomerang Bob trotting along on his leash. Neil felt really happy. Nothing came more naturally to him than walking a dog.

It was almost twilight. The sea was tinged with apricot from the setting sun, and birds swooped overhead. As soon as Neil let Boomerang Bob off the leash, he raced to the edge of the surf and stood barking defiantly at the creamy waves breaking on the sand.

"Gale! Come here!" a man's voice called from much farther down the beach. Neil heard panting breaths and thudding feet and turned to see the most fantastic dog running toward him.

It was short-legged and strongly built, with a stumpy tail. It had a long, wavy, gray-and-black dappled coat, a white chest, and a narrow, intelligent face. Neil couldn't for the life of him figure out what breed it was, but he extended a hand for the animal to sniff.

"What a great dog," said Emily.

"Hello, Gale. You're a beauty, aren't you?" Neil said admiringly, and the dog licked his hand.

Meanwhile, his father had gone striding across the sand and was talking animatedly to the dog's owner. Neil frowned, trying to make out what they were saying. That voice — he felt sure he'd heard it somewhere before.

Night was falling so quickly that, by now, the color had almost left the landscape, and his father and the

other man were little more than grayish shapes in the distance.

"Gale! Here, girl!" the man ordered, in the tone of someone used to being obeyed. The lovely dog froze, one front paw raised in the air, then turned and raced back toward her owner.

Then it clicked. Neil recognized the voice of the man who was illicitly exercising his dog on the beach.

"Em, Em," he hissed urgently to his sister at his side. "That's Frank Fitzbrien!"

"Are you sure?" Emily asked doubtfully. "It's pretty dark."

"Of course I'm sure," Neil replied confidently. "I'd know that big broad shape and that voice anywhere. So he lets his dog run free on the beach, does he? Think what we could do with this bit of info, Em!"

He couldn't wait to tell his father the man's identity. He was bursting with impatience by the time Bob Parker finished his conversation and headed back toward them.

"Gale's an Australian shepherd dog," he told Neil. "They're the most amazing creatures and —"

"Dad! Dad!"

"Neil, what's the matter with you?" his father asked. "You're like a cat on hot bricks."

"Yes, but I'm trying to tell you something really important. Guess who you were talking to!"

"Who?"

"Frank Fitzbrien! The man who's been keeping Boomerang Bob off the beach!"

"What? The man you keep calling 'Frank the Tank'? It can't have been!" his father scoffed. "Surely he wouldn't dare break his own rules? It's pretty dark. Are you sure you could see him from over here? Perhaps you're mistaken."

"I'm sure I'm not," insisted Neil.

"Well, I'm still not convinced," his father replied. "Why is he so tough on dogs if he's a dog lover himself?"

"He's probably afraid of getting fired," said Neil. "After all, there are lots of people who hate dogs."

"Jerks," said Emily under her breath.

Neil was quiet on the drive back. He was thinking how to use his newfound knowledge to his advantage. And, more importantly, to Boomerang Bob's . . .

The following afternoon, Neil and Jo stood outside the lifeguards' rescue hut and watched Harry the head lifeguard getting a crate of soft drinks out of his beat-up old car.

"Supplies for the competitors," Harry explained when he spotted them. "It's thirsty work rushing all over the beach in this heat. Still, it's the last day today."

"Could you get a message to Brett and Leo for us, please?" asked Neil. "Just tell them that their mascot will be close by."

Harry's brow furrowed. Then the man's eyes fell on the wicker picnic basket at Jo's feet. She had borrowed it from her mother. The cane strands were loosely woven, so plenty of air could get in.

"You mean . . ." Harry asked.

"Yes," confirmed Neil. "I think he's asleep."

"Good for you, mate! I'll tell them," Harry said. "I'm sure they'll be right along."

Neil and Jo found a spot on the beach and stuck Jo's beach umbrella in the sand to provide some shade for themselves and for Boomerang Bob, snoozing in his basket. They hadn't been there long when they saw Brett and Leo approaching. Brett had a plastic bag in his hand.

"G'day!" said Leo with a broad grin.

The two lifeguards crouched down and Neil opened the basket. The Jack Russell's shiny black nose twitched, his ears pricked up, and next minute he was wide awake and determined to find out what exciting tidbits Brett had brought him.

It was the remains of a hot dog. "He loves them!" Brett explained. The little terrier ate it with relish, then stood up and tried to push his way out of the basket.

"Sorry, boy, there's no more," Neil said.

He poured some water into a bowl and Bob thrust his muzzle into it, splashing the water out.

"Funny little tyke," said Leo fondly, giving the Jack Russell's head a pat.

"When do you go home?" asked Brett.

"Tuesday afternoon," Neil said. He had mixed feelings about it. He was desperate to be reunited with Jake, but how could he go home happily knowing he was consigning Boomerang Bob to an uncertain future?

"Hmmm — and it's Sunday today," said Brett slowly, looking at Leo. "We've really got to get our act together and find somewhere for him to stay, don't we?"

"Yes, you do," Jo said. "Our rescue center will be full for at least another week."

Neil and Jo watched the last round of surf carnival events at a distance from the rest of the crowd. They took Bob's basket off the beach at regular intervals, to let him stretch his legs and have a drink. But they weren't too far away to see the Dingoes give a magnificent display of their surfing skills.

The four Dingo lifeguards — two girls, named Pippa and Jilly, plus Brett and Leo — surfed in formation. They caught the edge of a big roller and stayed with it in a line all the way to the beach, their lithe bodies ducking and weaving as they kept their balance. Not surprisingly, they came in first in the event and Neil and Jo applauded like crazy. Their applause was even greater when the Dingoes also won the very last event.

Now that the surf carnival was over, it was time for Neil to meet up with the rest of his family, and for Jo to go meet her brother Alan, who was arriving on the ferry after a day out in Sydney.

"I'll just say good-bye to Bob before I go," Jo said, unfastening the basket.

The little terrier was wide awake and in a mischievous mood. The moment Jo loosened the leather straps that held the lid on, he pushed with all his strength, wriggled out, and scampered around them, barking happily.

"Come here, Bob!" Jo cried, attempting to grab

him. For a small dog with short legs, he could run very quickly. The Jack Russell raced along the shoreline, barking at the waves. Neil and Jo dashed after him, but each time they got close to him, Bob gave them an impish look and ran on.

"I think he's enjoying this," panted Neil.

"Stop that dog!"

"Oh, no!" Neil groaned. He recognized that voice only too well. Frank Fitzbrien was walking toward them, glaring. He was obviously off-duty, because he was wearing swimming trunks and sandals instead of his official uniform.

Bob darted away from the ranger and toward Neil, who held his arms out wide to grab him. But the terrier took evasive action, and sped off the beach and into the trees behind a café.

"I've already warned you once," said Frank the Tank, recognizing Neil from their previous encounter. Frank shook his head, still glaring, and went back to his beach chair.

"I'm really sorry, Neil. It's all my fault he escaped. I should have been more careful," Jo apologized.

Neil sighed. "You couldn't help it," he said. "That terrier's got a mind of his own. I suppose I'd better tell Mom and Dad so we can all go and look for him, or he really will end up in the pound."

Jo retrieved her mother's picnic basket from and sand and waved good-bye to Neil. They were hoping to get more surfing in the following day — the last full day of the Parkers' vacation.

But now that last day might be taken up looking for Bob. *If Boomerang Bob has made a bid for freedom,* thought Neil, *then maybe freedom is what he really wants — not a home of his own.*

CHAPTER NINE

Neil rejoined his family and told them what had happened to Boomerang Bob. They packed up their beach things and started to search for the Jack Russell — scanning the beach, looking among the trees, and even peering into all the nearby cafés to see if Boomerang Bob was begging for scraps.

There was no sign of him anywhere.

Reluctantly, Neil had to admit defeat, and they all headed back to the bungalow to shower and freshen up before they went out for dinner. It was Bob Parker's treat — a fancy restaurant in Sydney for which they all had to look their best.

At six o'clock, Bob checked his watch. "OK," he said, "it's time to leave. Everyone ready?"

Carole led the way. But as soon as she opened the

door, Neil heard a familiar noise. It was a high-pitched yip-yip that could only come from one particular tan-and-white Jack Russell terrier!

Neil and Emily both burst out laughing as Boomerang Bob trotted into the hallway, his stumpy tail wagging happily.

"I don't believe this," Carole Parker said with an amused sigh. "Just when you think you've seen the last of him, that dog turns up again. You certainly chose the right name for him. He really is just like a boomerang!"

"Neil," said his father sternly. "I want a volunteer to stay behind with Boomerang Bob. And that means

you. You'll be OK, there's some ham in the fridge. Although you might have to share it with your friend here. I bet he's hungry."

"No, we can't leave Neil here alone. I'll stay with him," Carole offered.

"And me," announced Emily.

"Me, too," said Sarah.

"So am I the only person who wants to eat a gourmet dinner in Sydney?" asked their father.

"Looks like it," Carole replied. She was hiding a smile.

Bob Parker grunted angrily and went off to call the restaurant to cancel their reservation.

"Did you really want to go?" Neil asked his mother as soon as his father had left the room.

She shook her head. "Don't worry about it. It was your father's idea. He said he wanted to try some Australian lobster because he'd heard it was delicious."

Bob returned with some good news. He'd also phoned King Street Kennels, and one of the rescue center's long-term residents had been offered a home at last.

I wish it could happen to Bob, thought Neil gloomily, reaching down to stroke the dog's head, now resting affectionately on his foot.

Carole and Emily volunteered to pick up some take-out food.

*   *   *

After the family had finished eating and Sarah had been put to bed, there was a loud rapping on the front door.

Carole thought it might be the real estate agent wanting to make arrangements for a last-day inspection and the handing in of the keys. She quickly dispatched Neil to hide Boomerang Bob somewhere in the garden while Bob Parker answered the door.

The visitors were Brett and Leo.

"I'm afraid we haven't found Bob yet," Leo said worriedly. They both looked crestfallen.

"That's not surprising," said Emily. "He's here!"

Neil was called back inside with the Jack Russell to greet their visitors.

The two surprised lifeguards laughed and made a fuss over Boomerang Bob.

Then Leo cleared his throat as if he was about to speak, but it was Brett who got in first. He was grasping a flat, square package.

"This is for all of you," he said, "to say thanks for looking after Bob for us and to remind you of Dingo Bay and the Dingoes Lifesaving Team."

"Can I open it, please?" Emily asked excitedly.

"Of course," said her mother.

Emily undid the sticky tape and the wrapping paper so slowly and carefully that Neil sighed with impatience. When the gift was finally revealed, the whole family gasped with delight. It was a painting of a pack of dingoes in the wilds of the Australian outback. One had its muzzle in the air and was howling at the moon.

"Who was the artist? It's very good," Bob Parker said.

Brett looked embarrassed. "Me, I must admit," he confessed. "Painting's my hobby. My mom said I should have gone to art school, but I decided there was more money to be made in designing computer software — that's what I'm studying now."

"We will treasure this. Thank you very much indeed," said Carole. "We'll hang it on the living room wall when we get back home."

"Now that you've found Bob," said Brett, "we'll take him with us. We know you're going home in a couple of days, so we asked our landlady if she'd bend her rules just this once. She agreed, as long as we find Bob a home before we go back to college."

"That's great! But does that give you enough time?" asked Neil.

"We don't go back for a few weeks yet, so that should be enough time to find him a permanent home. Don't worry, you know how much we love him. Harry does, too. We'll all do our very best for him," Brett promised. "Tell you what. If you give us your address, we'll write and let you know what happens to him."

Neil wrote it down for them, and Leo picked up the terrier. Neil felt another pang of sadness as the door closed behind them. He was very disappointed that he hadn't found a permanent solution to the little dog's problem himself, but he trusted the two life-guards and felt sure they wouldn't let Boomerang Bob down.

"I wish we were staying longer," Emily sighed on Monday, their last full day in Australia. "Then we could have seen Viola and Sporty again."

Neil was secretly glad that they weren't seeing Sporty again. The poor Kelpie's sorry state was too upsetting. And even though he understood Viola's reasons for not offering Boomerang Bob a home, he still felt frustrated because she could have made two dogs so much happier.

The family passed the morning at the Reptile Park. Neil had arranged to meet Jo and her brother Alan on the beach after lunch for a final surfing session.

The rest of his family decided to stay in and rest for a while. "We might see you down on the beach later," said Carole.

It was a hot day with a slight breeze, and Jo declared that the surf was perfect.

"The current's strong, though — the wind's changed direction. Don't go too far out," Alan said. "I'll be in the café, so stay where I can see you."

"OK. We'll just be over there," Jo said, pointing to a patch of sand near the ocean, in a direct line from the beachfront café.

They spread their mats and towels on the sand and went straight into the water. Farther along the beach, Neil could see a lifeguard perched on the wooden lookout chair.

Neil had no sooner waded into the water, clutching his board, than a big wave reared up behind him and knocked him flat. He sat up, spitting out salty water, and heard Jo laughing as she swept past him on her board. She had brought a different one with her today — a red circular board that she said was more fun because it twirled around like an amusement-park ride.

"Here comes a big one. Get ready!" Jo suddenly shouted.

Neil took a deep breath and flung himself forward onto his board just in time to catch the edge of the wave and ride with it as it roared toward the shore.

"That was awesome," he said when he'd gotten his breath back.

Jo gave her brother a wave to show that they were all right, then she and Neil plunged back into the water. They waded up to their waists and waited, jumping up and down to avoid being swept to shore before they were ready.

"Dad says the seventh wave is always the biggest, so let's start counting," said Jo. "We've just had three small ones. Here comes four . . . five . . . Oh, *help!*"

She squealed as number six turned out to be the biggie, then did a sideways flip onto her board to go spinning toward the shore, while Neil floundered and splashed about. He'd missed it. Never mind, there were plenty more waves where that one came from!

They decided to take a rest and went to join Alan in the café for a cold drink. Although it was mid-afternoon at the height of the Australian summer, the beach wasn't very crowded. It seemed to Neil that in Australia there was plenty of space for everyone and you could find a whole beach to yourself without searching very far.

As he sat in the shade sipping his ice-cold, fizzy orange drink, Neil daydreamed about how things would be if only King Street Kennels could relocate to Australia. They could build a rescue center big enough to house a hundred Jack Russell terriers, and a boarding kennel with all modern conveniences, even a swimming pool for the dogs!

"C'mon, Neil, race you to the surf. Last one back to shore's a wombat!" challenged Jo, dashing off again.

"See you later, Alan," Neil said, and took off at top speed to catch up to Jo.

She was in the water before him, paddling out with her surfboard.

"Give me a chance!" yelled Neil, struggling against the powerful surge of the waves.

Her answer was a sassy laugh — which rapidly turned into a scream.

Neil looked up in alarm and stared at the spot where he had last seen her.

There was no sign of her.

Then a giant wave spat out her board and sent it twirling into the air like a red distress signal in the clear blue sky.

Neil stood braced against the powerful surf, his mind numb with shock. Surely any second now Jo would resurface, spluttering a little, but perfectly all right? After all, she was a good, strong swimmer.

His momentary shock wore off, and Neil suddenly realized that he had to get help right away. But if he started running toward the lifeguards, he'd lose track of the spot where Jo had disappeared.

"Help!" he shouted. "Help! Over here!"

Neil leaped up and down and waved to attract attention. His eyes darted back to the ocean, scanning its rough, heaving surface. Something was in the water, a dark dot a long way out, reappearing and disappearing as the waves reared up. The shape was heading fast to the left, dragged by the current toward the rocky headland.

"Help!" he yelled at the top of his voice. If only the breakers weren't pounding so loudly. He jumped, shouted, and waved again, trying to catch the attention of the lifeguard on the lookout chair.

It seemed hopeless.

CHAPTER TEN

Neil stared around wildly and saw Alan leave his seat in the café and start running toward him. Then, with a huge sense of relief, Neil finally saw the figure on the lookout chair frantically signaling to somebody.

From somewhere else came the sound of high-pitched, hysterical barking. As small tan-and-white shape was hurtling toward him in a flurry of sand, and behind it came two tall running figures wearing blue-and-gold caps.

Boomerang Bob didn't stop when he reached Neil. He kept on running toward the rocks that stuck out from the headland. Then he came to a halt, gazing out to sea and barking frenziedly, as Neil, Alan, and the two lifeguards raced to catch up with him.

"It's Jo. She's been swept out!" Neil gasped, breathless with fear. "I think Bob knows where she is."

"I'm going in," said Brett. And with that, the tall, fit lifeguard plunged off the rocks into the water and struck out on his board in the direction where the Jack Russell's nose was pointing.

"It's OK, Bob," Neil said soothingly. But the terrier took no notice and kept up his hysterical barking.

"Jo, Jo — please be all right," begged Alan, clenching and unclenching his fists.

They heard the sputter of an engine and saw a rescue boat cutting through the water with Leo at the helm. Brett had almost vanished around the headland and was still swimming strongly. Then, as Neil watched, his heart thudding, he saw Brett waving to Leo. The boat swirled to a stop and Neil saw Brett pass a limp form up to Leo, then heave himself into the boat after it.

Leo turned the boat and headed for the rescue hut. Only then did Boomerang Bob stop barking. He left his place on the rock and scampered up to Neil, wagging his short tail.

"Good boy!" Neil praised him, patting his head and rubbing his ears.

Bob gazed at him and placed a front paw on Neil's bare foot. "Come on, let's go and see how Jo is," Neil said. He picked up the Jack Russell and followed Alan off the rocks and across the sand.

Aware that something dramatic was going on, a

small crowd had gathered near the lifeguards' rescue hut. Neil started to push through, but an arm thrust out and stopped him.

"Just where do you think you're going with that dog?" boomed a horribly familiar voice.

"My friend's just been rescued. I've got to see if she's OK. Let me *past*!" Neil said fiercely, doing his best to remove the strong hand that was clutching his arm.

"Give me that stray dog and then you can go through," Frank Fitzbrien snapped. "It's a good thing I like spending my days off on the beach, otherwise

who'd be here to see that the rules are kept?" He reached for the terrier.

Boomerang Bob gave a warning growl.

Alan had vanished. Neil was desperate to follow him and find out how Jo was doing. Too excited to feel any fear, he looked Frank the Tank squarely in the eye.

"How's Gale, your Australian shepherd?" he asked meaningfully. "She appeared to be enjoying her run on the beach the other night."

The beach ranger's face reddened with embarrassment.

"Now will you let me through, please?" said Neil, shrugging off the man's grip.

The crowd made way and Neil saw Jo lying on a surfboard, her head to one side and one arm above her head while Harry carried out resuscitation procedures. He stopped for a moment, checked the pulse in her neck, and carried on.

The watching crowd was silent and tense.

Neil put the Jack Russell down on the sand. He was desperately worried. Nightmarish thoughts passed through his mind — thoughts he tried his best to push aside. *She can't die — she can't! But she's lying there so pale and still . . .*

Suddenly, Jo coughed and spat out seawater.

She was alive!

It seemed as if the whole crowd let out a big sigh

of relief at the same time, and a few people began to cheer.

Neil suddenly felt weak and sat down on the sand. Despite the hot sunshine, he was cold and shaky, and he wished his shorts and T-shirt weren't at the other end of the beach.

Bob stood on his hind legs and licked his face.

"Thanks," said Neil. "You're a real star!"

Bob's attention brought a warm rush of life back to him. He stood up and saw that Jo was struggling weakly into a sitting position, aided by Alan and Harry.

"Jo!" called Neil, going over to join them.

"I was caught in a rip," Jo said hoarsely, her throat strained from coughing. "It was so strong, I couldn't break free. It just carried me away."

She started to sob. Alan wrapped his arms around her and gave her a hug. There were tears in his eyes as he thanked the lifeguards.

"You should thank this little guy here for showing us where to find her," Leo said.

"Yes, Bob's the real hero of the day," agreed Harry.

Just then, sirens screamed as an ambulance came speeding up to the crowd. Two paramedics ran up to help Jo onto a stretcher, but first she held out her arms for Boomerang Bob.

As she gave him a hug, Neil heard a camera clicking. He turned to see a bearded man holding a very professional-looking camera.

"Who are you?" Neil asked.

"Bernie Collins. I'm a freelance photojournalist. I was just passing by when I saw the crowd around the rescue hut and guessed there was an emergency," the man explained. "It's too late to make the evening papers, so I'll take the film straight to the newspaper office."

"I hope you've got some good pictures of the Jack Russell. He was the one who really saved Jo." Neil went on to tell the journalist the full story.

"Thanks, mate. Make sure you buy all the papers in the morning," Bernie Collins said. "You'll be famous!"

Neil shrugged. "It doesn't matter to me. It's Boomerang Bob's story, not mine."

The photojournalist headed rapidly for his car, leaving Neil grinning to himself. If Boomerang Bob's photograph appeared in the paper and the story made the little stray out to be a hero, then surely people would be clamoring to offer him a home!

Alan want off in the ambulance with Jo, after promising that he'd stop by later and let Neil know how she was doing.

"That dog deserves an award!" insisted a large lady in a pink dress from the crowd.

"Yeah. How about it Fitzbrien?" a man said. "Once the story breaks, this dog'll be a hero."

"Why don't you give him the freedom of Dingo Bay?" said another.

"Yes!" came a chorus of agreement.

The hulking ranger stood there in silence, listening and nodding while Boomerang Bob gamboled around, being stroked and patted by everyone. It was a truly wonderful moment for Neil.

"Is he really a stray?" asked the young daughter of the lady in pink. "He's so cute. What did you say his name was?"

"Bob," said Neil proudly. He could hear people all around him openly discussing whether they could take the brave little dog home with them right there and then.

Then Harry held up his hand for silence. "Thank you, everybody. We all know that Bob is a very special Jack Russell terrier."

"Hear, hear," said Neil.

"He was happy living on the beach with us lifeguards for quite some time," continued Harry. "But that was before our new beach ranger was appointed. He did his best to round Bob up and take him to the dog pound!" He stared meaningfully at Frank the Tank. "Now, I'm not saying that rules shouldn't be kept, but surely they can be bent once in a while, in a special case? And Bob is a special case, as he's just proved to us today."

There was an outbreak of applause from the crowd.

When the clapping subsided. Harry went on. "We happen to know that Mr. Fitzbrien is a dog owner and dog lover himself," he said. "Isn't that right, Neil?"

Neil took up the cue. "Yes. He's got a beautiful Australian shepherd called Gale. I met her the other night." He knew, and Frank knew, that he could have said "on the beach." Frank shot him a worried look and Neil found it hard not to laugh.

Harry hadn't missed the meaningful glances that had passed between Neil and Frank the Tank, and his lips were twitching in amusement. "I'm sure Mr. Fitzbrien will make an exception for this plucky little hero!" he declared. "I do think that he needs a proper home, but how about giving Boomerang Bob here the freedom of the bay and making him our official mascot?"

Frank looked around and slowly nodded.

People applauded and cheered.

Neil was astonished to see the enormous ranger's bronzed face break into a grin. Then he actually walked up to Bob, held out his hand for the terrier to sniff, and gave him a pat.

His bark's worse than his bite, thought an amused Neil.

"I'd like to adopt him," someone called out.

"We could give him a really good home," claimed Mrs. Pink Dress.

Harry shook his head. "I'm afraid you're too late. A new owner has already been found, someone with special needs, and Bob will have a very important part to play in her life."

Neil stared at the head lifeguard in astonishment.

This was the first he'd heard about it. Why hadn't Harry told him? Catching Neil's eye, Harry gave him a big grin.

Sensing that the entertainment was over, the crowd started to disperse.

Harry came over to Neil. "Sorry, mate," he said. "I was planning to come around and tell you and your parents this evening, but I had to say something now before someone snatched Bob up and took him home with them."

"Who's going to have him, then?" asked Neil suspiciously.

Harry's eyes twinkled mischievously. "I'll give you three guesses — and it's not me," he said.

Neil gasped. *It can't be. Impossible,* he thought. "Not Viola?"

"Yes," Harry confirmed.

"But how?" Neil asked delightedly, his mind spinning with questions.

"I actually live quite close to Viola's house. We often walk our dogs down by the lake. My wife does the morning walk, and she says it will be no trouble at all to pick up one more and take Bob with our three. And when I'm off duty, I'll do it."

"Have you asked Viola?" Neil wanted to know.

"Yes. After you told me about her and Sporty, my wife, Linda, went to visit her. She and Viola really took to each other. Linda thinks Viola must feel very lonely up there on her own. She needs friends to help her, and so does Sporty. With my family visiting her, and Boomerang Bob to keep Sporty company, I think everything will work out just fine. Viola's certainly willing to give it a try."

"That's the best news ever!" Neil exclaimed. "I can't wait to tell the others."

"Tell you what. I'll walk back with you and help break the news about Jo," Harry offered. Neil was very grateful. He knew his parents would be horrified to hear that Jo had nearly drowned, and it would be far easier if Harry explained.

Harry was right. After reassuring Bob and Carole Parker that the accident was nobody's fault, he passed on the good news about Boomerang Bob.

Emily and Sarah both hugged the little dog tightly.

Carole glanced at her watch. "I don't see why we can't take Bob up there now. It's only four o'clock."

"Why not?" said Bob Parker. We've got plenty of time to take him over there. Then, on the way back, we can stop by Randall Farm Kennels and find out how Jo's doing. What do you all think?"

Everyone shouted, "Yes!"

When the Parkers pulled up outside the big white house at Orchard Meadows they saw Viola dozing in a deck chair on the veranda. Viola woke up when she heard the Land-cruiser and waved. As she got up out of her deck chair, a black shape detached itself from

the cool shade beneath the chair. It was Sporty, looking very thin and a bit shaky on his feet.

"Look who I've brought!" Neil announced. He
opened the door and Boomerang Bob bounded out.
He raced up to Sporty, came to a sudden halt in a
cloud of dust, and extended his nose to the larger
dog. Sporty bent down and sniffed the Jack Russell.
Boomerang Bob sat next to him, his ears pricked and
his tail wagging slowly.

"I think it's going to work," Neil said to Emily.

"So do I," Emily responded happily. "Sporty looks
better already."

Neil took two dog treats out of his pocket. "Here, Sporty! Here, Bob!" he called.

The Jack Russell scampered up, with the Kelpie plodding slowly behind. Bob wolfed down his treat immediately, whereas Sporty buried his nose in Neil's palm and took the dog treat delicately. But he ate it all the same. *That's the important thing,* thought Neil jubilantly.

"I've got a treat for them myself," Viola announced. "A bone each from the local butcher's. Harry's wife got them for me."

"Can I give them their bones, please?" Sarah begged.

Viola let her, and Neil was rewarded by the sight of a Kelpie and a Jack Russell gnawing noisily in the shade of a tree. His instincts told him that from now on, life by the lake was going to get happier all the time. Not only that but, because they'd be staying in touch with Viola, he'd be getting regular news about both dogs.

"We seem to have a lot more luggage than what we came with," Bob Parker grumbled the following afternoon as Neil helped him load their baggage onto a cart at Kingsford Smith Airport.

"Well, we did buy a lot of souvenirs," Carole pointed out.

"And lots of copies of the local newspaper," Emily reminded her. The front page featured a picture of

Jo hugging Boomerang Bob, with Neil and Harry standing beside her. The headline above it read:

DOG RESCUES YOUNG SWIMMER

"I bet I'm the only one who's actually minus an item!" Neil joked. He had traded his King Street Kennels cap for one of the Randall Farm Kennels T-shirts the previous evening. When the Parkers had dropped by on their way home from Viola's, they'd found to their delight that the doctors had pronounced Jo fit and well. It was great news, and they all promised to keep in touch.

Bob Parker picked up Neil's blue sports bag. "This

is kind of heavy," he said suspiciously. "Are you sure you haven't got a dog in here?"

As Neil joined in the laughter, he decided that this had been his best vacation ever — thanks to a very special Jack Russell terrier!